♥♥

Love Yourself(ie)

Life Lessons for Building Kid Charisma™

By Andrea A. Lewis

A Collaboration with Nicole Pearl

♥♥♥

♥♥

Dedication

This book is for all preteenagers growing up in the digital age, and the parents, caregivers, teachers and youth advocates who care about your happiness and well-being. May you know that you are amazing and that anything is possible with self-belief, determination and resilience.

Special Thanks

Special thanks to Nicole Pearl, The Beauty Girl, for her suggestion to spotlight self-love as our best accessory.

♥♥

Contents

♥♥♥

What we think about ourselves matters most.

♥♥♥

Chapter 1: Oh No!

"Did you see Charlotte's post?" Mia texted to Harper. "She looked amazing. I wish my hair looked that perfect. ☹"

Harper's friends loved to post selfies of themselves looking good. Not Harper, though. To her, posting selfies was a popularity contest, and it often left her feeling bad about herself.

"Yeah, I loved her shoes and my hair is totally jelly – LOL," Harper texted back.

Harper ate her last bite of dinner and went to her room. This Friday at school was *Fashion Day*, and everyone was starting to post sneak peeks of what they would be wearing.

Max posted a sunglass selfie. Sophie did a duck face in bright pink lip gloss. Even Jackson, who never posted about anything but basketball, took a baller selfie in a new hat.

They all were a hit, too. In just 15 minutes, each post had more than 40 'likes', and girls were asking where to buy the lip gloss.

Harper thought, "My turn!" She had gone shopping with her big sister, Madeline, over the weekend. Not only did she get trendy boots, but she also bought super cool earrings.

She decided to post a selfie only showing the earrings. First, though, she needed to clean up from dance practice. She showered, dried her hair and glossed her lips perfectly. Remembering how good Charlotte's selfie looked, she decided her hair needed some waves. About 45 minutes later, she was done.

"Now, do I want to show one or both earrings?" she thought to herself. Harper figured the best way to decide was to take selfies both ways. She didn't like the first one and deleted the second immediately. Finally, after 10 tries, she chose a profile selfie showing one earring. She loved it!

♥♥

"Sparkly fun for Fashion Friday! ♡,"
she posted.

Then, she watched…

At 1 minute, nothing.

At 5 minutes, 2 likes.

At 20 minutes, a comment: **"pretty!☺"**

At an hour, only 7 likes and 1 comment.

"Oh no," she thought. "Nobody likes it."

Harper's heart started to pound, her cheeks flushed and she felt sick to her stomach. She had worked so hard to buy something cool, look pretty and take a perfect photo, and yet only eight people, total, had something nice to say.

All of a sudden, Harper felt very unsure of herself. She took the selfie down and cried herself to sleep.

Chapter 2: Love Yourself Most

The next morning, Harper walked into the bathroom she shared with her sister, her eyes puffy from crying.

"Hey, what's wrong?" asked Madeline, who was getting dressed for school. "Nothing," said Harper.

"Come on, tell me," said Madeline. "There's no way you're fine with those swollen eyes."

"I feel left out," Harper responded, her eyes filling with tears again. "No matter how hard I try to fit in, I'm not liked as much as other kids in school. I don't know what to do anymore. It's crushing me."

"Well, that's the problem," said her sister. "Take a deep breath and get dressed. I want to tell you a story on the way to school."

As the girls began walking down the street, Harper could hardly hold up her head. Madeline put her arm around her and said, "Hey, most everybody goes through something like this while growing up. Do you know that?"

Harper looked up and glared at her sister, not believing 'Miss Popularity' was ever not liked.

Madeline continued: "When I was your age, my friend's brother said I was the ugliest girl he'd ever seen… in front of a huge group of kids. I was totally humiliated. Here was some boy who didn't know me, saying something cruel to make his friends laugh. For a while, my feelings were really hurt. Then, mom said to let it go. Pretty or not, I shouldn't let him or anyone else make me feel less than them or bad about myself. Well, guess what? She was right. Years later, this boy and I went to the same school. He, apparently, didn't even remember me because he asked a friend who I was and said that he thought I was beautiful. Can you believe it? I was so glad I hadn't listened to him."

Harper was quiet for a moment. "How could you just ignore it?" she asked. "Didn't that bother you? When I post a picture, everyone sees it and knows what everyone else thinks. How can I not care if they don't like it or, even worse, say mean stuff?"

"It *did* bother me," said Madeline. "I just decided that his opinion was not the one that mattered."

"What do you mean?" asked Harper.

Her sister looked at her and smiled. "Harper," Madeline said warmly, "love yourself!"

"What?" asked Harper.

"Love yourself," Madeline said again.

"You have your self-esteem wrapped up in a photo contest, and you need to reclaim it. Some kids fit in and some don't. Some kids are kind and others, especially girls, say mean things or act as bullies to get their way. So, focus on what you can control – which is *your* opinion of yourself.

Believe in yourself. Like yourself. Be comfortable with being you, and don't let what people say, or don't say, change how you feel. You are good enough just as you are, and anyone who doesn't agree isn't a real friend."

Harper stopped walking. "That makes sense, but it feels like it would be really hard to do," she said.

Madeline raised her eyebrows and looked Harper in the eyes. "It *is* hard to do," she said. "Not letting others influence bad feelings or behaviors is a choice, though. If you want this, you *can* do it!"

Chapter 3: Wait, What?

Harper went through the day watching her friends while thinking about her sister's story and advice. Some kids were chatting and some were only bragging. Some seemed happy and others uncomfortable. "Where do I fit in?" she wondered. "I've always cared so much about what others think of me. How do I stop?"

After school, Harper decided to look through photos and find ones that truly made her feel good. To her surprise, they weren't perfectly posed selfies. Rather, they were photos of silliness. Coming across a ridiculous picture of her wearing an old dress of her mom's, Harper thought: "Madeline is right. I have to be brave and focus more on what *I think* of me."

And just like that, with her heart racing and a lump in her throat, Harper nervously posted the picture.

♥♥

"What not to wear... fashion disaster! ☺"

To Harper's complete surprise, kids went crazy for her post. It was the exact opposite of what everyone else was doing, and yet within minutes she had lots of likes and comments.

"Wait, what?" she thought. "That's not at all what I expected. Wow. Amazing. I guess I really can do this."

Just then, Mia texted: **"Hey, ♥ your selfie!"**

"Me too," thought Harper. "Me, too."

Made in the USA
San Bernardino, CA
30 May 2016